Thank you for taking the time to read this book,
I appreciate you and that you considered
buying this book. Thank you.

Selected Poems
2018 - 2023

Table of Contents

Cancer

The steel sarcophagus I lay in
mother clutched the cerulean gown adorning
my body
close to the poison needle where I found no
hope.
far into the night, my pulse was made audible
like musical psithurism on a summer day,
I the wind, brought a hush to that music
and a tear to those eyes that gave me life.

Kids in pain

A stranger in the mirror.

Razor fresh with blood, and you think

"Why?", you watch it unfold

hoping for a sign.

It's not you, you're just there for the ride

buzzed hair, falling down the drain.

ugly inside and out.

And you wonder, "Why do I see what I see?"

not comprehending any answers, as if lost in
translation

somewhere along the way.

Lost like a child in a house of mirrors.

Your baby cousin is so adorable.

And I am left with a strange feeling
having been in homes
meeting brothers and sisters of men who no
longer call
getting glimpses into futures I am no longer a
part of
hungry for that promised dinner downtown
and to hear from your mother,
your baby cousin won't be tucked in tonight
my palms are here, not there.
yours are elsewhere.
You're fine with that
it makes me hate you, and cuts me downright to
the bones
somehow I don't belong in any of your futures
and it is all just a memory.

Sweet child

Her head weighed next to nothing
pulling the blue duvet over her.
Her little eyes finding mine.
In that gaze she relays a message,
she trusts that the floor will not give, that the
walls will stand.
The fridge and the cupboards will not be empty
and as she begins to rest,
she sleeps with the comfort that I will still be
here
to pack her lunch and to brush her hair the next
morning.
That she will have a home after her classes
end,
that I will be there with her.
Every step of the way,
supporting my child.

Turning

I fell into a deep sleep,
when I woke up I couldn't tell the difference.
There was nothing to distinguish it.
The days were all the same, time was just time.
Watching the world pass by, and for a second I
thought I must have been dead
maybe everyone was dead I thought.
The world was very much alive however.
I could tell by all the motion, all the cars moving,
all the noise in the distance.
I watched, I listened.
The noise was so nauseating. There was no
break, no silence.
The moving never stopped, moving, moving
all day, all night.
Everyday there were people moving but it was
all pretty much the same.
People moving without going anywhere.

Partners

You break my heart
when you get like this,
all boozed up and broken.
It breaks my heart but I would never leave
telling your mother i'd look after you,
so don't make me a liar.
Because i'm tired of watching you throw your
life away.
Getting too drunk to handle.
I'd lay eyes on you blacked out on our bed
Thinking about how to fix the state you're in.
So I will pour my heart out some more,
again and again until you listen.

Crying in the dark

Another night, spent in a dark room
silence, ringing in the ears
thoughts pulsing.
Eventually consuming everything
frightening away any sense of calmness
breathing thick and difficult
as if the air were thinning,
no longer natural
no longer unnoticed,
a thick chest and suddenly
something has taken a hold on you,
and in that darkness you can feel everything
coming all at once
violently, like a flood
like the hurtle of the ocean,
like falling without a parachute
or the force of a raging bull
pinning you down
gasping for air.

After us

At first, every person looked like you,

every car I mistook for yours.

Relationships never felt the same.

Frightful to what trust can do.

I didn't know how to fix it

this haunting feeling,

of a ghost from my past.

Whether I like it or not,

I had to learn how to suffer,

to move on.

Savoring the moment

Somewhere in time
we knew one another
but I could never get back to us
and I will never get a chance to see a future
with you and me
and as it rains
I think about you
the way it pours
reminds me of your balcony
at night, when it drizzled
as the cars would pass by,
how gray clouds illuminated your face
your eyelids closed, peacefully asleep
making everything black and white like an old
picture.
as if saving the moment for a rainy day,
for when you would no longer be here.

Walls

As the walls of your home,
and the grass, and the trees outside
watch on
like the mirror perched on the wall
or the canvas hanged over your bed
that sees your naked self like no other
truly some recognition of moments unforetold
some self that is never realized
clothes hide the person within the person
where do they go at the end of day
when the faces are made, the actions, the
words aren't from that inner person?
A self within,
buried but not dead.
It's something worth weeping over,
somebody never allowed to live

Moon

It's not dark out,
yet I can see the moon
and the birds flying away
against the trees the bugs lay
gentle wind blows, windows are open with
nightstands holding lamps; People are moving
around, the sounds of cars can be heard.
A sun kissed sky with blue hues
and I wonder when it'll all end,
I can hear it, I can smell it, a breeze hits my
face, my mouth still has the taste of cigarette.
My stomach growls, my body grows heavy
looking out as far as I can see
As minutes fill the hour,
as an hour passes,
it is dark now, and I wonder when it all ends.

Time passes

When all is said and done
my time had been spent well
hunger pains for what I had not yet done or
been,
we're now replaced with a fullness so
comforting it could lay me to rest,
but the day is young and I have time left over.

Just maybe

It wasn't easy,
I gave no reason to believe in me
the way that you do.

The love you give is too good for me,
at least that's what I think
because I think very little of myself.

And you, you see me for me
you see that I can be loved,
and it heals me.

You're bad for me

The hand to beat me
same one that raises me up
yet I stay, some impulsion
a feeling, the sensation
of being unfit for another life.
Behaviors of a messed up kid,
falling for abusive partners
self inflicted they call it.
And yet I get no say.

Thank you

Living cargo, bled dry like steak blood.

A dollar here, a dollar there. A drop in the
bucket.

Ringing of phones, purrs of radiators in
cramped apartments, honking of cars

insatiable hunger, appetite for prosperity

and an empire unfamiliar to stillness.

A latent image to the dream for which my father
had

before crossing over, singing prayers of better
times.

For his family, prayers to stay afloat among a
slew of bills crashing down on him.

Neutralizing fear, committed to a dream while others stayed stuck

that predatory way that poverty does.

Just because…

Just because you shut the door
and turned off the lights
doesn't mean I can't see you.
even at night
when you pull the covers over your head
shutting your eyes.
I can still see you.
when you drive off in your sedan
to somewhere empty
the woods, the plains, or an empty lot
I am still there
and you can play your music,
listen to those videos you find yourself smiling
over
you will still have me in your ears.
no prayer or drug will stop me
you can hide in the crowd, blending in
you can try, and you will fail
I promise you that.
just know when you find yourself happy and
content
joyous in your circumstances

my words will still hurt.
In times of hardship
many have heard my voice.
when the broken are gone off the deepest ends
I appear, when sickness provides
and I've followed them to their graves,
some earlier than others,
just as I will follow you, listening, watching.
So you can try to get rid of me, but you will fail
I promise you I am still there.

In a dark place

The only sound was the ticking of her clock, it seemed natural

some flowers, a few pictures here and there.

She'd stand then sit, pacing around

the house mocked her,

it was hers but she felt estranged.

She could hear her heart throw a tantrum.

No tears escaped her sad eyes, though she wished they would.

Some release, for how lonesome it all was.

She stared at her phone, without much people to call

or who checked in, only the fridge and
television called her.

Times like these she prefers to watch
something and eat.

She would think back

on all the people who would come and go,
along with her happiness.

It was hard to deal with the impermanence,

relationships were so fickle she thought

because something stable seemed
unidentifiable.

Her hope would come and go.

Fearing the day it just goes.

Late into the night she'd rustle around,
occasionally picking up her phone and putting it
away.

Sleeping a few hours each night.

Thoughts teeter tottered,

suicidal, pessimistic, and self doubting.

A restless mind, always looking for the faults
wherever they could be found.

She would blame the world, she would blame
herself, she would blame god.

After coming home from work,

she'd sit on the sofa staring at her carpeted
floor, hosting a debate in her mind.

Thinking who's to blame for all this pain and
shortcomings.

Spiraling,

until she finds an old movie and begins to play
it, falling asleep to it.

The day passing, the week now over.

She hoped tomorrow everything would be alright, promising herself

she would not break down this time.

Letter

I found your letter in my drawer as I was
cleaning
and I paused to read it,
in every sentence,
I could hear the anger as you explained how I
had hurt you
kicking you to the curb, making you feel
worthless
how you stayed up thinking of me for nights on
end,
I didn't remember this, maybe I didn't want to.
Your words hit me deeper now then when I was
younger,
perhaps time helped to feel the weight of my
actions, now I see that I was wrong.
Believing myself the victim.
Being selfish without realizing it. Pushing others
away,
ruining you, I see I have not changed in my cold
ways
though I want to, and for what it's worth, since I
didn't say it then

i'm sorry for hurting you.

I long to be home

It is Wednesday. I think.
Winds warn me of rain, or maybe snow
the clouds rolled like black and white film
and melancholy misted over adolescence.
Classrooms were full, leaving houses empty
and a longing for the comfort
of the place each child called home.
Cocooning oneself in blankets creating
a weightiness similar to a hug.
TV's play, lulling many to a gleeful state
only to discover they had fallen asleep when
they are awoken for dinner.
It is Wednesday at school
and I long to be home.

happy day

Open fluttering, a butterfly on a still day
and god is content with the creation of it.
You can tell by the yellow and tame orange
surrounding everything
that nothing is wrong
the warmth of a happy day
washes over, carrying you away
and you are made new.
The butterfly passes by
as if to say, "I Love You"
you reach out open handed
as if to say, "I Love You Too."

Fifty or so

A raging ocean
crashing an oil tanker
killing fifty or so,
earth spun in silence
unheard in its deafening glory
too big to last or to stop.
Without enough time
to save one another
when the debt collector comes.
Asking forgiveness with dirty hands
water no longer pure
and our hands no longer clean
wanting more
the oil fields pump blood
and the earth keeps spinning.

wait…

The wait,
begets longing.
A prolonged suffocation
and the burning
of tears.
How terrible.
Never will I be the same.
All that I do
you would not do,
for me.

Nimble

Speaking quietly,

silently crying.

Only I knew.

Heart too nimble to break

ripe with embarrassment.

Strong enough to go on,

too defeated to change.

Painful to watch,

though my eyes wouldn't look away.

My brother slipping into submission.

Never leaving my thoughts, how I had lost
someone

by watching them lose themselves.

Boat in the ocean

Ever there was a time for you to speak
it would be right now,
watching you was like looking at a man
struggling to keep their head above water
during the thrashing of a storm
in the middle of the pacific.
And how badly did I want to save you
to pull you to safety, aboard my small boat
so that we could ride out this storm together
and even as I reached for your hand,
you never grabbed it.
Even as I called your name
you turned to face the sea
and I knew then there was no saving you.

Cheap diners

There is an evil in me
a blackness in my lungs
coughs that are nasty. People see me and keep
walking.
Nobody ever stopping, nobody ever
acknowledging this old face.
Sitting in cheap restaurants eating my daily
meals alone.
No family, no children, no friends.
No freedom to start over, for I am too old.
There is no more laughter being shared,
no one to hear me speak, no one who wants to
see me
and I am afraid I'm dying alone.

Silhouettes through the day

Time eluded the forfeiting sight

invasive to that third eye, only leaving
silhouettes

of some former self

as if time had finally caught up.

Providing prescriptions

grainy and gritty.

With someone so beautifully damned

who sees the world in disgust,

only looking forward to a recliner and a can of
beer.

Pollen

Everflowing beams of sun onto green,
connecting souls like bees to pollen.

Rain from earth and sea,
feeding into our soil creating luscious trees.

Beauty in our existence.
Grain for you and grain for me.

Sharing with me your planted seeds.
Evolving past evils by a world more equal.

Mundane

Mundane is the day.
Today I exist
and I am okay with just existing.
The motions let me know…
That nothing is wrong.
A peace I've grown to appreciate.

dance with me

Dance was essential
a ceremony for courting.
Coordination had no place in spontaneity's
court.
It really didn't matter how bad you were,
so long as your brain didn't dictate.
So long as you were free, you could dance.

today

Today's morning was brought into existence,
solely to greet you.
Sunrises are there to witness something more
beautiful than itself.
And
sunsets are created so you can miss all that
you love.
Moon cycles reflect your brilliance in the dark
giving shape to the cycles of life

I'm no shakespeare

In vain these efforts to be good,
diverged from where I should.
Weight my name do carry,
a devil my veins do carry.
Embalmed by duplicity,
brings a great shame
thy name I bear.

Tomorrow

Tomorrow lies my faith.
Surrendering myself to that,
Happily I say "Today is over"

saying farewell to the joys and misery
of yesterday for new ones
when tomorrow comes.

Stories being written
every moment passing
and I want to write page after page

always another page
to replace the last

as if it were some great story.
For when tomorrow never comes.

Moving time

Someplace familiar,
white walls with cheap paintings, finding
unkempt grass because it had grown too long
breezes blowing aroma's of earth after a
downpour of rain
a stretch of rock that stays youthful,
seeing aged faces, yet still familiar

where nothing special came or went
except for amusement parks in the summertime
yellow buses filled with children that pour out in
the afternoon
parks that know everyone, and everyone knows
them
families went through life here, it's the place I
know.
it's the town that raised me, some stay and
some go.
Hard to let go of your home when being there
feels familiar.

Wardrum

Head to chest
ear to heart
he played
a wardrum.

Coffee

Life had the potency of black coffee.

Staining pearly whites,

searing roofs of mouths.

Needing sweetener, at least

for those who hate the bitter taste.

It was so each morning began that way,

with a cup of coffee.

Misty

It was nice seeing you,

but I would have preferred visiting you at your
home.

Still, it never left me.

The smile from the thought of you is still there.

You were dear to me.

You gentle soul, even with wrinkly misty eyes

you never aged a day.

When I was just a child

how you would play with me.

Bits of you that were gifted and

passed down.

Make it as if you never died.

Dandelion

Morning came

peeking over the horizon, the sun

bringing light to a rose garden.

In it, a single dandelion.

Never had I seen a dandelion among roses.

Reliving in silence

Laying, screaming, crying
nobody came to stop it.
Eventually it was all over
no longer would I yell
forever hiding
beneath my skin.

Friend

I tell you to leave me on the floor in my
drunkenness.
Yet I wake up on your couch knowing damn
well you carried me.
Nights when you had no one else to call
you call me,
days when we have time to kill we pass the
time joking around talking about everything
even the not so important stuff.
I swear I hate showing my face anywhere I
don't need to, but it's bearable to go out and
have a laugh together.
You give me your time, it shows that you find
some happiness here.
Out of a whole room at any given place, on any
given day, I wouldn't trade you for anyone.
Even when I forget myself, even when I get lost,
you recognize me.
Fear sometimes pushes me away, telling me to
keep to myself
but you find me
the way lost family members do

with open arms.

Crumbs

Not enough to eat
not enough to get full
just leftovers.
The pieces thrown into the garbage.
You get crumbs
and the hunger pains
are enough to make a person curl up
ready to die.
A gnawing in every minute that passes by
crumbs won't help
not even a little
but it's all you got.

Loser

Suffering alone like most men
mistaking loneliness with pride.
Afraid of the mirror
trying foolishly, giving up
only to try again.
Falling and falling
never hitting the ground.
Consumed by time
like a dripping candle.
Oh what a loser I've become!

I'm fine

I wanted you to think everything was fine.
Deep down I thought of you.
I missed you,
every night I couldn't sleep
without thinking if you found my replacement.
Filling the empty ME shaped space left
on your bed.

Letting go

Nonexistent words formed a hard boiled egg
in my throat. Scouring for words.
Stiffened air with nothing said
silence was a floating catalyst for grief.

Silence the mourners understood.
Before descendance
hesitant last words of goodbye were mustered.

Letting go killed me,
standing there above your grave so incomplete
and I wish I could give you everything I didn't
before.

Hour

An hour is all I ask,
time out your day
to reconnect with you.
An hour is all I ask

Even that is too much.
Understanding as I am, urging myself to be
patient
Waiting like a fool, in hopes for you.
Until I realized I am not as important to you.

An hour a day is too much for you,
it's just as much an hour of my day too.
You can have your hour back, but
I won't give you any more of mine.

I will try

Cry to me that you need fixing and I will try,
push me away angry and afraid.
Like a rubber band stretched I'll throw myself
back or at the very least I will try.

Hospital beds, disappointed parents, and
judgmental looks
certain doom claw away any hope,
yet I remain.

My face anguished, eyes holding back tears
from years between us making me question if
this was really worth all the effort.
Only to see good in all these years. To make
you happy
to ease your pain, I will try.

Ugly

God doesn't like ugly,
but it's not god that doesn't like ugly
it's people.
I see it in friends who try to include me in their
conversations about who they're seeing
or who they like,
listening with nothing to say.
I see it when I go to dances alone,
when the messages I get never make my heart
race,
when I eat meals for one.
People hate ugly,
people don't flirt the way they do my friends,
unless it's for the night.
People don't think of me when they lay awake
imagining their romantic fantasies came true.
People don't come up to me when I sit alone
because people don't like ugly.
People like pretty and perfect smiles, they like
pedestals, they like prizes.
People don't see me, but I see me
and I hate what I see.

Arguing with myself

He's always been there, arguing
dragging my legs down numerous hallways like
a drunkard not wanting to go home
finding flesh to lay against.
Dirtying sheets, spurring about hope of a
forever on earth;
Too many forevers to feel the same faith in it.
Yet inside I hear a voice negging me on, to give
it one more go.
-Give it one more try
it says without ever actually saying a word
yet after so many people I always lay alone.
Sometimes it lasts for months, weeks, days, a
night.
I have come to expect this.
Laying awake arguing with myself
until I'm exhausted,
only in my sleep is where I find
a forever on earth.

Necessary

I got tired of people reading the surface
just to believe they know me
it's a shame, that I
am dismissed purely by a bio.
Trying to not go insane
from all the dead waste
rewarding attention grabbers
with slight fame.
Over sexualizing ourselves,
swiping left or right.
I can't remember any memorable
conversations.
Being overfed or underfed our daily needs,
what a shame.

Lousy

There's always labor to be done,
he's not a smart man.
Working early, waiting for the day to end.
Waiting for his lousy fix of beer and whatever's
left in the fridge.
Watching tv before washing up, staring at the
mirror.
White hairs on his head, without a care.
Wearing old clothes that ought to be replaced
Inhaling his cigarette
warming his lungs, smoke drifting away leaving
its taste.
He knows he will die a sad death
aware of his sad life
it's no secret.
There is no beauty here, it is simply his time.
So he sits there
he will wait.

Shopping for cereal

My favorite of all cereals.

Mom knew how much I loved lucky charms,

though there was something off today.

It was subtle at first, was there some stain on
my shirt?

Toilet paper on my shoes?

Maybe my hair had become wild, it was humid
after all.

That wasn't it either, my mother didn't seem to
notice or just not care.

I brushed it off as one of those strange days
you can't quite describe.

Two weeks later my mother and I went
shopping again,

lucky charms as usual. Some ham for dinner,
then it hit me as we were checking out.

Some random guy between 16 to 17,

I didn't know him but he eyed me, up and down,
before looking away.

It was quick, I looked down and didn't see
anything unusual.

Except my breasts,

fifteen and I had the world out to get me.

My body had betrayed me.

I began feeling uneasy, growing uncomfortable.

Since then when I go out for groceries, I feel
less joyful buying lucky charms.

Old in age

I don't feel okay,
the reality is sickening.
I wanted time,
but there would be no more time.
I wanted to tell everyone,
that I was right and they were wrong
but it was always the other way around.
I thought that I was meant for something grand
the truth is I am an ordinary man, living an
ordinary life.
Life had no big plans for me.
I had big plans, dreams that excite
then I lost them, too in over my head.
I was young once,
that is neither here nor there.
Somehow time slipped away.
I was happy once,
that too slipped away
then I stopped looking forward, and looked to
the past.
Seeing regret in all I did and didn't do.

Damp walls

Rain beat down the weathered roof
consequences of spring,
a moldy ceiling. Rain leaked through,
dampening walls.
The youngest sits on the carpet watching
cartoons,
her older sister plays homemaker cooking rice
and chicken.
Waiting for a woman in her early thirties,
Smoke trails from the bus, their mother stepped
out.
Wearing a thick coat. Steam from dinner filled
the kitchen
a smile appeared on that little face, as she said
"Dinner's ready!"
The youngest hugs her mother, and they all
take a seat at the table.
They shared a meal, talked about their day,
the girls were tucked in,
the woman undressed and showered before
going to bed.
She laid closing her eyes,

dreaming wide awake of a bigger house,
of better pay, of cooking for her children not the
other way around.
A tear streamed down her cheek, unable to
avoid crying
Opening her eyes to mold on the ceiling.

Evil created

Absent from light
similar we become.
Suffering the illness of hatred
destined to an eternal life of sin.
Piercing through skin a fiery scorch straight
from hell.
A man's wounds may heal but there's no
recovery from death.
My gun flies up, no future, no present, and fire
back.
Look into my eyes, can you see? The new bred
evil.

young once

How does it feel,
oh to be so excited?
To simply be,
to live life as if you had all the answers,
yes I was once young.
But I was never like this.
Perhaps that's my regret.
Too have been young
without living
or wrongdoings to learn from.

Four legged friend

She can be heard down the street
her eyes wide and tail wagging excitedly,
as if it were some grand reunion.
My four legged friend was barking up a storm
i'm sure the neighbors loved it.
Scratch sounds from the door as I entered.
She was so excited to see me again
even I don't get so excited at the sight of a
friend
but it feels good.

Sooner

One day I will not be here,
and the world will keep spinning, the trees will
keep growing,
the wind will never to hear my voice again.
Grass will tickle feet of children as they run and
play,
rain will continue to fall.
Flowers will bloom, fruit will ripen
the sun will shine, the moon will still come out.
One day I will be put to sleep without ever
waking up.
Just gone,
one moment there and the next gone.
Just like that,
people will go on living.
Once here on this earth. Smiling, crying, hating,
loving.
Searching for something that I may never find.
Good days and bad days,
a moment, a memory,
just a memory, hopefully a fond one.
Sooner or later I will be gone.

Beautiful dream

The windshield wipers squelched,
the turn signal clunked,
lights flashed yellow.
- ...so what'd you dream of?
A green sedan passed by, splashing through a
great big puddle.
- I dreamed of us laying in bed, in the
morning...
- I opened my eyes and I saw your face next to
mine. So I smiled, and tried to go back to sleep.
But I guess I must have woken you because
you asked if I was awake, I groaned and said
yeah.
- I opened my eyes again, you were staring at
me with your green eyes and the sun looked so
pretty on you. We kissed and smiled then we
just laid there next to each other.
- That's when I woke up. You were sleeping.
The light turned green.
- That's a beautiful dream.
We drove through a great big puddle in an
underpass

- It wasn't a dream.
I smiled at her

Held

A weight, burning
Like scotch through my chest, as her arms
tightened.
Held while I could be,
I did not think,
Solely this moment.
Letting me know how she felt
That we are thick as thieves.
Fools of fate,
Players of our cards,
Gamblers, who are
Nothing without risk.

Somewhere and nowhere

Dirty laundry piled up,
cries without tears
and a headache striking
like nails into my head.
Something refused to leave this
weakened spirit, unable to exit the room.
With curtains closed, where I have been
reduced to a shell and withdrawn.
High from medications, relief without control
turned off from the world never leaving the
radius of the one bedroom apartment.
Time was slow, an empty hole. It was
inescapable, it was cruel.
Food became repulsive so I stopped eating
keeping my demons full instead,
preventing myself from getting any better.
Finding myself between somewhere and
nowhere.
No courage mustered to head out that door.

It goes and it goes…

I can't help myself,
I can't help but wonder about my life
and why we cannot start again,
or why silence is so maddening
or how the night makes me feel so alone.

How my eyes stare at chairs and wonder why
they're empty.
How we focus on pain so much, rather than
letting it go.
How everything is off in the distance, all our
dreams and wants.

Waiting for the day we get there
awaiting to be released from our desire.
Thinking thoughts, that never leave my mouth

Never to see the light of day, never to leave my
mind.
My heart too excited, pounds itself into an ache
Waiting for that day.

It's funny that way

- There will always be more people but there
will never be more time
- You can go and find someone else, and I can
go and find someone else
- But what's the point?
- If I can't decide that i'm going to stay with you
and stick things through then it really comes
down to what kind of person you are and what it
is you want
- Because the next person isn't going to be any
different
- I love you, I love you and that's not something
I can change
- And I choose to stay with you because that's
what I want. I want this.
- I want to be here with you. With all the
possibilities of a future with you.
- Some people, yeah they fall in love for a
month and then get bored and some people fall
in love and they say yeah this is nice, I like this,
this is what I want. Because love gets boring
and I get that. I understand it's not always going

to be exciting but I want to be with you
regardless, and that's my choice. Because this
is what I want, and I don't regret it.
- But just because you want it doesn't mean
someone else wants it just as badly as you do
He chuckles
- It's funny that way.
She looked into his eyes.
Holding his face, her eyes wide.
- I want this too. I believe in us.

My Freedom

People can be themselves,
I just want to see the individual
that knows themselves.

Where entertainment and temptations of daily
life and words of others don't reach me unless I
want them to.
But I don't want them to.

Where I am free,
not rich and not poor
just enough to be happy and content with
myself.

Not held down
by the worst in me
or by the worst in others,
just free.

Your hands

I promised to watch you walk the aisle
some day in your own home town.
Years later here we are,
you gave me your hand my mother's ring sitting
pretty around your finger.
Gold and silver with a diamond
taking your hand,
in reverence to this feeling of something more
than myself
feeling obligated
to not disappoint.
Dignified and strong
in your deserving hands
with rigid legs and fire in the chest
how complete I stood
husband and wife.

Never again

I never realized my own worth, and it stuck.
Seeking approval other than my own.
How small the world became
running into someone like him everywhere.
After the let downs I thought I would let go
easily.
But it hurts being alone, so much I rather be his
and I am convinced he is the only person for
me.
Yes he convinced me,
but my heart knows it's wrong.
And I don't love him, and he doesn't love me.
He used me for his own self worth
if he loved me he wouldn't make me second
guess myself
or make me feel guilty for telling him how I feel.
I deserve better.

It's gonna be a long day

The worst days are the ones you can't see
coming.
Where you don't know your own footing,
the days…
You might not recover from.
When light is not at the end of the tunnel
and the days have no end in sight.
When you adjust for an uncomfortable next few
hours, days, maybe weeks.
The worst days make you
despite the chance that there is no end.
Against the dying day
waking up to zero,
fighting against it all.
You only know it's gonna be a long day.

Mortality

Mortality showing its face, I wondered, what
purpose did I serve?

Creaking of floorboards as I traveled to the
kitchen

Passing framed photos from a lifetime of raising
a family,

it was the only noise in this house.

There were birds, how she loved the birds

and her garden. I could only watch on, waiting
for something to happen.

Then I heard the cat meow to tell me she was
hungry.

I poured her bowl full of cat food,

finally shuffling through the carpeted floor to the
living room.

An old sofa of a blue suede.

Sitting there felt off without anyone.

A pretty woman in a long summer dress caught
my eye,

sitting on the table an old photo from before I
was married or had kids.

She smiled, and it was as I had always
remembered her.

Overwhelmed with joy and pain of forty six
years. I sobbed,

the house no longer quiet.

Stale people

Well, the house was payed off

and the days were all the same.

A routine driving to and from work,

cooking and cleaning. There was love between us,

it had just gotten so tame. No fights, no scares,
no illnesses or deaths.

The furniture never changed, dates were stale.

Our friends were free of drama or issues of their
own, it irked me.

No surprises even on my birthday I felt the
same as any other day.

We had fun traveling in our 20's, when we
struggled to make enough.

Saving up for flights and hotel rooms we couldn't yet afford.

Reminiscing on when love was uncertain, so I could prove it again and again.

Now the proof is that I am still here each day, the way I let her shower first whispers

"I love you" unlike when we first met and we couldn't keep our hands off each other,

each kiss was new and exciting.

I guess 30's are supposed to be when couples turn stale.

Big John

Every now and then

when I sit alone getting drunk

I think of the cowboy who sat on the balcony

smoking with a drink in his hand.

Even in his absence

I still see his long drags

bringing stillness to his face.

Smoking, drinking, young, and scared

but I'm no cowboy.

My sorrow was present,

it showed on my face and slumped shoulders.

Days like today where I fear that nothing is
enough,

I know somewhere that cowboy is sitting in
silence

With stillness, stoic like

and that seems like enough.

Medicine cabinet

The cabinet shelves were lined with goodies,

uppers and downers to last the week.

Some were prescribed.

None of them I really needed,

but who's to say.

It sure beats booze,

it was a science to me

finding the perfect mix.

Telling nobody, yet everyone knew.

Sweating all the water out of my body

as if I wasn't already drinking too little of
anything already.

Eating here and there.

My focus was meeting with my dealer,

or getting home fast enough to grab more.

I scheduled my day this way.

Skinny and high,

I was unstoppable.

2 am gas station

Her pajamas had some dirt around the ankles

the man at the register stared,

her hair with all its flyaways looked raunchy.

Her crop top was brown, her pajamas black
with pink slippers and a purse

It was better than staring at the neon signs
outside

and less depressing than staring at homeless
people sleeping on the corner.

Watching as she looked around,

Wondering if she has a boyfriend

She goes up to him

- Did you find everything okay?

He asks

-Yes

She says reaching in her purse.

He wants to ask for her number, or her name.

To escape such mundane mediocrity, but all he musters is

- That'll be nine ninety nine.

She pays and leaves.

The gas station employee is left staring out the glass door at an empty parking lot.

Chance at redemption

Due to poor circumstances,

you can find me curled up in the driver's seat of
a 1998 sedan,

sun too bright to handle with open eyes,

it was the end of the month, I was dreading the
next.

I was worried I wouldn't make it, or that I'd
barely make it through.

Worried my apologetic self would start to grow
tiring on those who forgive me most.

The house wasn't enough, neither were the
promises I had made.

I needed a better job, a better house, more time
to spend with my wife.

Yet when I opened my eyes and saw myself in
the rear view mirror,

I found it too daunting.

So I closed my eyes again trying to forget my reflection as the sun beat down on me with its heat.

I begged for my chance at redemption, to lift my head up to face life.

Play something

The song wasn't that good,

but it was catchy. The beat was pop

maybe rap, by this point I can't tell the
difference.

The lyrics were pretty bland, the words were
just words.

My friends are not gangsters or murderers or
living in section eight

so I don't know why they play this music on car
rides to a nine to five job,

I don't know now

and I won't know later what exactly is being
proven.

Little moments

These moments that are mine,

heighten my senses.

On a long road trip,

hiking through rocky mountains

feeling my joints as they ache

telling me my age. Waking to sounds

of my kids playing in their tree house.

Drinking coffee early in the morning on the porch

thinking about little things more than I normally would.

So when I observe, I merely watch these little moments.

They are not planned,

yet they're perfectly timed.

Memories

There are things we can never explain

no matter how long we reflect.

Things that we will forever remember

without ever being able to go back to it, except in your mind.

Smells, tastes, sentiments that will pinpoint a time and place.

Names to faces, a feeling that stayed with you.

Memories are all a person has.

Flawed man

On hardwood floor, pleading to god, I was met with denial.

Looking for pleasure I only found pain.

Up or down it was all the same,

just an ignorant man making ignorant mistakes.

Still I stood, a man.

Staying earnest while walking the line

hoping it will lead somewhere

where I can find some peace of mind.

Flesh

They will turn on you,

lie and make you feel as though you are to
blame.

They will find ways to get under your skin

causing you to react in ways that feel so
manipulated.

People will cause you pain

only to offer pleasure right after.

More vile than anything in existence,

they will eat your food, take your belongings,
leave you out to dry.

There is no loyalty; when it grows inconvenient
there is no loyalty.

We are flesh disguising the monster within

quick to turn, quick to ridicule

but nobody likes to be turned on

and nobody wants to be ridiculed.

Beaten then caressed all by the same hand

just flesh and bone with no direction.

Believe me

Where did everyone go

after I opened my mouth?

I could do without my friends

it was not being believed that pushed me over
the edge,

the few that did kept me sane.

But why were they scared to be around me
now?

Why do I suffer sleepless nights being called a
liar?

It was hard to admit I had been abused,

it was lonely when nobody wanted to share the
embarrassment.

Being a victim was embarrassing,

yet the one that did this to me walks free and clear.

Even the family members hate me for ruining their precious child's reputation

Maybe it's easier to believe I'm a liar to them,

but where does that leave me?

It's hard doing what's right when nobody else does.

Is this the treatment for those that refuse to be silenced?

If so I will take on this uphill battle

I will not be tossed aside,

I will not be silenced.

Just a game

Dawn's cold breath brings back memories of childhood.

When my mother worked long hours,

the days all seemed the same.

Snowstorms meant no school, and slush that made you slip.

Despite lacking any real substance

those days mean the most to me now.

The snow still falls, but it doesn't feel playful anymore

and Christmas films fail to deliver,

the house is sitting empty.

Snow meant play

before bills and expectations

when all I had to do was live carefree,

when life was just a game.

Destiny

Fighting to change my reality

escaping fate.

Days became markers,

milestones to strive for.

Day after day

counting away how long i've gone on

without playing chicken.

Finally changing my destiny.

Season

From this valley,

beginnings and ends.

Pricked and pruned, my life forgotten.

Roots forever planted in the earth,

skin godforsaken

a distasteful bark.

A valley with critters and birds

granting shelter, extending my branches up
above

showing leaves of a misjudged love.

For sun and rain call the bloom of life,

creating everything anew.

Long, i've yearned for my turn in the showers of the season.

Certain deed

Nothing is certain until the grave is filled

no person so hopeless that they are best
forgotten

no deed left unsung even if by your own voice.

No feeling buried alive ever died,

no matter how far light travels forth.

No day passes without miracle or tragedy,

no color can't be found from the rising sun.

No day ends without a tomorrow.

No, there is hope.

No it may not be here but it's somewhere.

Appalled

I blame society

for failing human beings

and creating monsters,

acting appalled

when they act accordingly.

I blame parents

for their deaf ears and blind eyes

creating children that are no longer children

that destroy themselves

when they are unheard.

I blame the teachers

each day a child is no more than a student.

I blame the nine to five worker

passing by the panhandler without a single
word

when they ask for change.

I blame myself

for not doing a thing,

when there is so many problems to go around.

A peaceful quiet

A peaceful quiet

where even my own voice won't find me,

my greatest moment of bliss.

Relief of being unabridged.

An animated shell of flesh and muscle,

fat and hair.

Without desire to be more than I currently am.